ALL I WANT FOR CHRISTMAS IS BOO

A FINAL GIRLS FEATURETTE

TYLOR PAIGE

For the Whorror Babies who need horror with their romance all year round. Merry Christmas.

This book is also dedicated to Sia, whose Christmas album inspired this book.

FOREWORD

Hey! So, first off, I hope you enjoy All I want for Christmas is Boo. Please consider leaving an honest review wherever you do reviews when you're finished. If you do, tell us what rule was your favorite. Honestly this book is so fucking bonkers, I don't even know where to start. Maybe the icicle stuff?

Now, to cover some bases.

Spoiler alerts!

This book is *meant* to be fast paced, absurd, and, a nod to home invasion horror. If you think too hard about the world and the logistics, you lose the fun. Yes, I am aware of how electricity works, or that icicles melt, etc. Just roll with the fast pacing, keep reading, and just enjoy the book for what it is, a spicy horror romance. Thanks, whorror babies.

THIS BOOK IS RATED R

All I Want for Christmas is Boo is a horror romance novella with topics that can be upsetting, uncomfortable, and for some, triggering. I encourage you to consider this list to know exactly what you are going to see while reading this book. This story features noncon, body betrayal, agoraphobia, public mass murder, graphic murder, anxiety attacks, home invasion, violence featuring guns and knives, masked figures.

RULE 1 - LUMEN

USE ALL YOUR SENSES TO IDENTIFY THE MASKED MAN.

"**P**uppies are forever." I shook my head, turning away from the large, glass window where the most adorable dogs were dressed in bows and playing with a ball. A sign above them said "Take me home for Christmas." I fought the urge to go inside and pick one out. "I'd rather go to the pound. Plus, I'm not ready for that level of commitment."

Shy, my sister, sighed. "You're not ready for any kind of commitment, which is the problem." She tugged on my arm, and she and my other sister, Tauren, walked past the pet store and on to another clothing store in the mall.

"I was ready for commitment, if you remember—" I started, but Tauren cut me off.

"Please, do we have to hear this again? Ben was a loser. You are lucky, in my opinion, that he called the wedding off."

I flinched, and just then, as if on cue, a Mariah Carey song started playing over the intercom. I covered my ears and let out a cry of anguish. I couldn't escape it.

Shy, my sympathetic sister, frowned. "Well, the most

famous song being played every twenty minutes probably doesn't help the situation. Or this."

All three of us stopped short at the giant poster on the wall ahead of us.

MAREY CAREY: IMPERSONATOR LIVE THIS WEEKEND!

I stared at the image of the girl who stole my future from me. Dressed in all her Mariah Carey- wannabe Santa outfit glory, she was smiling so wide, as if she wasn't a home-wrecker.

I pivoted. "Let's go get a pretzel before I tear down every wreath and Christmas light in this place."

"Actually"—Shy looked at her watch and exchanged a look with Tauren—"we had an ulterior motive for coming to the mall today..."

"Have you seen the ads for those *blind date photoshoots*?" Tauren grinned. My stomach dropped, and I shook my head furiously.

"Tauren, no. You didn't." I panicked as I looked across the mall, zeroing in on the photography studio on the other side.

"You have the new lingerie." Shy pointed out, her eyes dropping to my red bag.

"You made me buy these!" I protested, but then it hit me. "You planned this all out, didn't you?"

My older sisters smirked and pushed me toward the business. I fought with my words the entire time, trudging past Marey Carey's poster. It had been almost a full year since we'd gone to her concert, where my fiancé promptly dumped me after, confessing that they'd been having an affair for months.

We stopped at the entrance, and I stared at the poster advertising the blind date photoshoots.

Let's shoot your shot at love.

"Lumen?" A goth girl with a large smile and giant blue eyes came out, a camera hanging from her neck.

"That's me."

My sisters urged me to go in. "Go have fun," Tauren smiled. "We'll be back in a few hours. Let us know if he's hot or not."

"Come back at three!" The photographer grabbed my hand and tugged me along. "I'm Neve, and you're in good hands."

Changing into my brand-new, rather racy, red lingerie, I was handed a silk robe and sent to a hair and makeup artist.

"Do you know anything about who the guy is?" I twisted my fingers in my lap. This was my first official step toward moving past Ben. And, if I was honest, it was long overdue.

"His name is Tobias. He's twenty-two, and he's yummy," Neve teased.

"Yummy?" I raised an eyebrow.

"You'll see." She played coy, and soon enough, I was staring at a version of myself I'd never seen before. Neve frowned. "Are you okay?"

I pressed my lips together. "I've just... never looked this pretty."

She gasped. "Oh honey, no. You're gorgeous without the makeup. And that body? Tobias is going to lose it when he takes his blindfold off. Now come, he's waiting."

A silk blindfold was tied over my eyes, and she took my hand, leading me deeper into her studio. "Okay, be careful. There's a bed, a chair, and some props we can play with. You two are in complete control here. Consent is key. If you want to stop, say stop. Are you ready for Tobias to come in?"

I took a deep breath. No amount of preparing would calm my heart. "Yes," I whispered.

A moment later, a door clicked open, and I heard footsteps.

"Hello," a deep voice greeted me. Flutters erupted in my belly, dripping down to my core.

Oh.

"Hello." My voice came out shaky. "I'm Lumen."

"I'm Tobias." He came closer, and I leaped out of my skin as large, warm hands fell on my arms.

"Good, now, explore each other," Neve said softly, reminding us that she was there. She began to click furiously, and I blushed at the knowledge of being watched.

"Is this a robe?" Tobias asked, his hands sliding down my arms.

"It is." Tentatively, my hands reached out to touch him, finding his chest. He wasn't wearing anything on top, and his muscles were chiseled. I gasped. He chuckled low.

"Is that a good gasp?"

"Very much so." I sighed, running my hand down the middle of his abs. I counted the muscles, all eight of them.

"Can I get rid of this?" he asked. His hands drifted from my arms to my waist, and he tugged playfully on the robe strings.

"If you want to." My words were breathy, getting lost in my throat.

"I do," he said, pulling the robe open and pushing it down my shoulders. I shivered as goosebumps appeared from the chill air.

"What do you think?" Neve asked. "Is her body to your liking?"

4

Tobias ran his hands down my curves. I wasn't Mariah Carey curvy. In fact, Ben had thought I was too thin, but I kept an hourglass figure. His hands reached my hips, and then dropped, going to my face. The scent of his cologne invaded my nose, and my body melted, savoring the manly scent. It was musky and minty and... smoky.

"Are you smelling me?" He chuckled.

"I—Well, I can't see you. I'm relying on my other senses."

"Good girl," he muttered, sending my mind spiraling. His voice was an aphrodisiac in itself. "You've already used sound, scent, touch. What's left?"

My heart was beating so loudly I was sure the room could hear.

"Taste."

Suddenly, I could feel his face close to mine, and I parted my mouth as his lips connected with mine. My brain exploded as endorphins flooded my system. His lips were soft, and I could taste the mouthwash and faintness of a cigarette. He tasted like he sounded.

"You want to move to the bed?" Neve asked us. We were so wrapped in each other, I was deaf to her constant clicking around us. Tobias took my hand and led me to the bed. I crawled onto the silk sheets and felt the pressure of him joining me.

"What are you comfortable with?" he asked gruffly.

"Uh, I don't know?" I couldn't admit to two total strangers that I had zero experience with this. It was the exact reason why Ben left me for a Mariah Carey imper-sonator.

You're too frigid. I'm not waiting for you anymore.

"How about Tobias take the lead, and if you get uncom-fortable, you tell him to stop?" Neve suggested.

"Okay."

A moment later, warm hands were on my thighs, trailing up my body. Lips replaced his fingers as he moved, and my legs relaxed, parting. He moved between them with expertise, and his kisses fell onto my belly, then my breasts. I gasped as he pinched a nipple, sending delicious shivers through me. He found my lips again, and he added his tongue this time, eliciting a moan from me.

"Lumen, you're fun." He chuckled, pulling away. "Have you done anything like this before?" He trailed kisses down my body, and I shook my head furiously.

"No, never!"

"Good answer," he growled, and suddenly, as his lips found my thighs again, my core began to ache.

"Wow, your chemistry is..." Neve muttered, then cleared her throat. "Are you ready to meet each other face-to-face?"

He moved away, and I sat back, biting my lip. What if he wasn't what I pictured in my head? My hands went to my blindfold.

"It's okay. Let's count down. One, two, three."

I untied my mask and my eyes darted to the figure in front of me. He was the hottest man I'd ever seen in my entire life. Time stopped as I memorized his face. Hair so dark, eyes so blue, face so chiseled, lips so... mine.

Is he as pleasantly surprised as I am?

"What do you think?" Neve asked.

Tobias grinned and lunged at me, running his tongue along my neck and pressing his lips to mine again. Neve erupted into laughter. "Yes! I knew you two would click!"

We finished the hot and steamy photo session, and I slid my robe back on, suddenly aware of how exposed I was. Tobias smiled from across the room.

"So, can I give you my number?" he asked.

Butterflies swirled in my belly. That gorgeous man wanted to talk to me again?

I nodded, then realized I didn't have my phone in the room, so he wrote it on a slip of paper and I folded it up.

"I hope you call..." He hugged me politely, as if we hadn't spent two hours making out. I nodded and hurried to get changed and return to my family. Mom and Dad were probably irritated they were stuck waiting for me. My sisters might not have informed them of their plans.

I was just finishing putting my shoes on when screams rang out from outside the studio. I grabbed my bag and flew out of the shop. People were screaming and running every which way.

"What's going on?" I screamed over the others.

A woman paused to stare at me in horror.

"There's someone with a knife. Four people are dead at least!"

And as she fled, the knowing dread of who those four were froze me to the floor.

RULE 2 - LUMEN
FIND A GOOD HIDING SPOT.

One Year Later.

Pink. Purple. Yellow. White.

I stared at the Christmas lights flashing on my tree, mixed in with the silver and gold tinsel, and random ornaments. So bright, meant to bring holiday cheer, but all I felt was... melancholy.

Pink. Purple. Yellow. White.

I pulled my knees up, wrapping my arms around my legs. What was the point?

My doorbell rang, and I frowned. My heart twisted as anxiety rose. I slowed my breathing and reached for my tablet to check the camera. Relief flooded through me, as I saw Billy, the delivery man.

I dropped my feet to the floor and hurried to open the door and greet him.

"Lights are up!" Billy beamed from the porch. Despite him decked out in winter gear, his cheeks and nose were flushed.

I crossed my arms over my sweater, leaning against the

doorframe. "William Watanabe, you really didn't have to do that. No one's going to see them but you."

Billy was the only real friend I had anymore. After my family's murders, I took the insurance and moved out of my city in lower Michigan, going north. Far north. I found a nice cabin in the middle of the woods, in a town with almost no people, close to the Upper Peninsula. It was perfect.

It was safe.

"True." Billy grinned and rubbed his thick gloves together. "But I like seeing them on my daily visit."

Visit was a hyperbole if I ever heard one. Billy had never even been inside my home. No one had.

We met the first time when he delivered my groceries I'd ordered online. And then after a month of weekly deliveries, he began to bring me my mail from my mailbox, a mile down the road. And the daily letter retrieval turned into packages or random coffee from the local bakery.

"Did you decorate your house?" I asked.

"A little. Although after getting zapped a few times from your old-as-dirt lights, I'm a little hesitant to climb a ladder to do my lights." He laughed.

"I'm sorry. They're the same ones my dad bought before I was even born."

His smile turned into one of sympathy. "Then I'll gladly put them up every year. A little electrocution never hurt anyone."

Silence fell between us, and Billy, as always, felt compelled to fill it before I thanked him politely and shut the door.

"Christmas isn't really a big deal in my family. Even though my dad has never even been to Japan, he insists on doing what they do over there, and eat fried chicken and this thing he calls Christmas cake. He claims he wants to return to our roots, but my family moved here in 1890 or something. Way before KFC ever was a thing. I like to go ice skating over at Lochary Lake sometimes. The ice is thick enough now if you want to check it out."

He was rambling.

"Billy, I adore you, but it's cold. Thank you for doing that for me. Even though I won't see them, knowing the lights are up is comforting. My dad would have liked that." I stepped back and began to close the door. "I took your advice. The tree is up. Maybe it'll help..."

I doubted it would make me feel better about being utterly alone in the world, but it was a nice idea.

"Wait!" Billy put out his hand, stopping the door. "Can I see it?"

I shook my head quickly, an electric bolt of fear flashing through my spine. "No! I mean..." My face flushed in embarrassment and guilt.

Billy was the only person I'd seen in almost eight months. The overwhelming dread that came over me every time I was in a public place sent me spiraling into panic attacks so hard I would often collapse or break into tears.

I hadn't left my house since I moved, and I hadn't let anyone inside either.

What if he had a knife?

I stepped back, far enough so that he couldn't swing a hidden weapon and hit me.

In an instant, I'd been completely orphaned by a mass murderer. There were eleven of them. All innocent mall patrons, happy to be shopping for the holidays. He killed with abandon that day, and later laughed, at the trial, when they brought out photos of his victims. The fear of it happening to me consumed me to an unhealthy level.

"Billy, I don't know if I'm ready for that," I said what I said every time he hinted that either he come in or I come out. His face fell, and I gave him a tight smile, and my gaze drifted from his friendly face to the snow-covered yard. I looked up. It was starting to snow. Everything was so... clean, so fresh, so new.

Maybe it was time for me to open myself up to new things.

Billy dropped his arm, and I opened the door a bit more.

"What if..." I paused, inhaling deeply, steeling my nerves. I closed my eyes.

You can do this. Billy is good people. Billy doesn't want to hurt you. Billy doesn't have a knife.

They found my parents and sisters only twenty feet from the photography studio. It appeared that they had been waiting for me to get done when the killer turned down and rushed them. They put up a fight, but he was fast and was able to stab them each multiple times before they could flee for help. Dad had gotten the worst of it. He had tried to cover my sisters and Mom to shield them.

I left the mall alone and hadn't been back since. It wasn't safe anymore. Nowhere was safe.

But Billy is safe. Inviting him in can be the first step.

I opened my eyes and stared at him. Yes. I could do this.

"Christmas is in three weeks. How about Christmas Eve, you come over, and I'll make cocoa, cookies, and we can watch Christmas movies?"

Billy's face lit up, and he thrust his hand out. "You've got a deal!"

I leaped back as instant fear hit me like a brick to the face. My face flushed with mortification as Billy stared at me in concern.

"Oh, Lumen, I'm sorry. I didn't mean to scare you. I was just—"

"I know, you're fine. I-I'll see you later, Billy." I went to close the door again.

"Are we still on for Christmas Eve?" He leaned to see me.

"Yes. Let's plan for that." I bit my lower lip hard until I could taste blood.

"Great! Oh! I almost forgot; your mail. I picked it up for you."

I paused as he dug into his pockets and pulled out two letters and a folded manila envelope. I took it from him cautiously, the fear of him grabbing my wrist and pulling me outside ever prevalent in my mind. Who was sending me stuff?

"It's the season," Billy said, as if reading my mind. "Probably one of those oversized Christmas cards."

"Maybe. Thank you, Billy. I'll see you tomorrow." I shut the door quickly so I didn't have to see the deflation in his face as once again he was shut out. I spun around and rested my back against the door and then bolted away, the fear of a large knife penetrating the wood and slicing me in half forcing me to lock and flee the entryway.

I went to the kitchen to sit at the island and open my mail. The letters were junk mail. I looked at the front of the envelope. *How strange.* It was addressed to me, with my old address, so it must be someone I knew from my previous life.

When things were happy.

I pulled out the contents and gasped. I blinked and dropped the photos onto the countertop. I hadn't even thought about them since that day. How hopeful and happy I'd been afterward. I stared down at the photos of me and my handsome stranger, Tobias. With shaky hands, I picked them back up and began to go through them. The photos were stunning and had my heart racing. I ran my finger across his lips, and sadness overtook me as I remembered that while I was kissing this unfamiliar man, my family was being murdered.

Everything happened so fast, I'd lost his number.

Not that I would have called him anyway. My life now was depressing and embarrassing. Who would want to be with someone who couldn't leave the house without sobbing uncontrollably?

I reached for the envelope to search for the address of the studio. I would have to write her a polite thank-you letter. She probably had no clue how much it hurt to see these but was just trying to be kind.

But as I flipped the envelope over, I discovered that not only was there no address listed under my name, there wasn't a return address or stamp either.

RULE 3 - TOBIAS
COLLECT ALL EVIDENCE OF YOUR CRIMES.

"Creme Brûlée Cappuccino for Tobias!" the barista yelled my order and set my cup on the counter. I stood, pausing to set the envelope I'd received a week prior on my table. Getting my coffee, I returned to the table and stared off into the distance while I waited. I glanced at my watch. I was told to be here at two, and it was five minutes past.

A moment later, the bell above the door dinged and two women came in with loud stomps and shaking to get the thick snow off their boots and coats. She didn't have to remove any of her winter gear for me to know it was her I was waiting for. Even in winter, she wore black, head to toe.

The pair of women hung up their hats and coats and then went to the counter to order themselves something to drink. I watched intently, sipping my drink, as they moved through the line, gushing to each other as if they were just here for a friendly little catch-up.

Hardly.

Neve turned to look around the cafe and spotted me,

waving excitedly, as if the mail she'd sent me wasn't straight blackmail.

This town was... quaint. I'd grown up here, but left the week after I graduated high school. I only returned a few times a year to visit my dad, but I hadn't been back since last year, after the tragedy at the mall. Eleven dead in an hour. Four of them right next to the studio I was in all afternoon.

"Tobias, how are you?" Neve and her friend slid into my booth after picking up their steaming cups. "How have you been?"

"Fine," I replied curtly, sipping my coffee. While I hadn't had plans to be in this shop today, my drink was good. "And you?"

We'd attended school together. I wasn't much for friends, but we ran in similar circles. I hadn't hated her then. So when she called me up and pleaded for me to apply for her photography thing, I did it. And, surprisingly, I'd had fun. But that was a year ago, and things had vastly changed. Now, I wasn't interested in being friendly.

Neve slapped her hands on the table and widened her eyes. I took note of her appearance. She'd put a ring through a nostril since I'd seen her last. Her eyes were still the same startling blue, so pale they were almost white. With her pale skin and black makeup, it made them stick out even more.

"Could be better." She laughed loudly, causing people to turn and stare at us curiously. "I mean, my boyfriend is in prison for the murder of eleven people, and my business is in shambles now because they believe my work was what caused his mental break, but hey, it's Christmas."

I remembered the articles and the news. While I didn't stick around afterward, Dad had been obsessed with case.

He'd sent me daily updates about every little thing. I vaguely recalled an article about Neve and her photography business. They'd villainized her for "promoting pornography" because of her boudoir photos, and the blind date photoshoot we'd done. Sex, drugs, and rock and roll, were the whole reason Kane, her wannabe rockstar boyfriend, did what he did. Or so the media said.

"This is Ruby, my partner in life and crime." Neve put her arm over Ruby's shoulder. I turned to look at the other woman. She was the total opposite of her girlfriend. Her hair was long, straight, and a ruby-red color. Her makeup was mostly modest, highlighting her brown eyes, except her lips which were a cherry red. Her clothes were very... pumpkin spice, MLM, boss babe-esque. I only knew the words because my last fuck was one just like her. She'd gifted me so many herbal lotions and glitter vitamins.

"Well, one of them, anyways. You're going to be added soon."

"To which one, exactly?" I asked. I looked her up and down. While the goth look was hot normally, my favorite streamer was a goth chick who made tea and cupcakes all day. Neve's appearance did nothing to my dick. Not even one little throb. It never had. "Because I'm not interested in someone who sends me shit like this." I pushed the envelope with the damning photos inside.

"Oh, it was just a little joke. Come on, can't we all use a good laugh after the year we've all had? I'm sure your life isn't all rainbows and sunshine being on the road all the time, doing what you do with all those animals."

My mood turned cold in an instant. I preferred to keep my life private. I didn't exactly welcome her knowing things about me, like my address or career, which, apparently, she did. I doubted she truly knew what I did for a living though. If she did, she wouldn't be so bold.

"Oh, calm down. I saw your dad at the store and we caught up. This town doesn't change much, even with a little murder."

"Can we hurry this up? I'm supposed to be visiting with him for the holidays. Why did you send me these?" I slid the folder across the table. Neve's smile widened, sending a small shiver of uneasiness through me. In a flash, the smile turned into an exaggerated pout.

"I thought you'd want the photos of you and Lumen. That day was pretty memorable."

I nodded. Before the murders, that day had been... something.

I'd never been that instantly attracted to someone. Especially one I couldn't see. Lumen had lived rent free in my head all year. She'd become an obsession I couldn't get rid of. These photos were evidence of that.

"Yes, but why now? You could have given these pictures to—"

"The police? They did ask for them. But I respect my client's privacy, and as they had Kane on camera in other places around the mall, they didn't need these."

"Are these the only copies?" I asked, knowing they weren't. Neve wasn't stupid. Neither was I.

"They can be. If you help me."

I cocked a curious eyebrow. What did she want?

"I want revenge. It was Lumen's testimony at trial that sent Kane to prison."

"He went on a murder spree," I replied.

"Yes, but he only killed seven people. And we both know who killed the other four, don't we, Tobias?" Her eyes darted to the envelope containing damning evidence. I gulped.

"What are you thinking?"

"Oh, nothing much. It actually took me a bit to track her down. The bitch fled town. Pretty sure she was too scared to show her face after so boldly lying about what she saw."

"Why do you think she was lying?" I'd watched the video of her testimony. She'd told them that she'd seen Kane run past her, covered in blood, and coming from the hall that her family was lying dead in. That was it. She was on the stand for very little of the trial.

"Because Kane never went that way. But someone else did."

She reached for the envelope, and I snatched it. Neve was unhinged. She was going to show these photos to the whole cafe.

"Anyways, she ruined my life. Kane is in jail for life, and my career is completely ruined because she lied. Now, we're going to get her back. She doesn't deserve all that money her family left her. I do."

I looked from her to Ruby. What were they proposing? Ruby rolled her eyes.

"Lumen lives up north, way up north. She's all by herself, and she's got money. We're going to rob her," Ruby rushed.

"And you're going to help." Neve spread her hands across the table. I stared at her, clocking her jerky movements and dilated pupils. She was high on something.

"And why is that?" I snickered. By the looks of her, I could easily do some digging and find the original photos or videos and take care of them. I wouldn't let her go to the police with what she knew. Neve smiled wide again, and I decided then that I would make it my mission to wipe it off her face permanently. But it was her words that pulled the smile from mine.

"Because I know that you're in love with her. If you don't help us, I'll give Lumen the photos showing you killing her entire family."

I glared at her.

"What do you propose exactly?"

Neve dug into her large bag and pulled out a mask. She offered it to me, and I took it gingerly, examining it.

"You're gonna need this."

RULE 4 - LUMEN
MATCHING PJS ON THE FIRST DATE? RED FLAG.

The oven beeped, signaling that the next batch of cookies was done. I left the garland I'd been hanging up and went to the kitchen to remove the cookies and put another batch into the oven.

Billy had mentioned that he had no favorite cookie, so I was making him all sorts. I'd been following my favorite streamer, *Witchful Drinking*, all month long while she baked for the holidays. She and her boyfriends were so fun to watch, and she made following along with her recipes so easy. I plopped peanut butter cookie dough on a cool tray and slid it into the oven.

Returning to the living room, I glanced at the TV and smiled when a commercial announced that the A Christmas Story 24-hour marathon would begin soon. Which meant...

My doorbell rang, and my heart simultaneously sped up with excitement and terror. I hurried to the door and peered out the peephole. I breathed a sigh of relief as Billy's face showed on the other side, slightly warped but smiling.

I waited until my heart settled to put my hand on the door-knob and turn it to welcome him in.

"Merry Christmas Eve!" Billy shouted, startling me only slightly. He thrust a metal tin into my hands. "My mom made a Christmas Cake. She's not much of a baker, but I promised I'd bring it." He stepped inside, and I froze.

This was all happening so quickly. I stared with my mouth half open as Billy took his coat up and hung it on the rack. He stomped the snow off his boots, and every step caused me to jump. It was a lot of things all at once. He turned and smiled.

"You going to shut the door? It's a bit cold." He chuckled. I shut the door, locking it. I then unlocked it and locked it again. What was I doing? This wasn't me. I hate the fearful person I'd become over the last year. I took Billy in and relaxed.

"Those are adorable." I grinned, taking in his holiday pajamas.

"You like? Good, because I got you a matching pair." He dug into his coat and pulled out a small red and green shimmery bag.

"You did?" I gasped, as I opened and found the matching teal PJs with snowflakes all over. "Oh, Billy, that's so sweet! Thank you." I went to hug him, but hesitated. There was a moment of awkwardness as we took in my fumble. I stepped back and looked to the floor. "Well, I should go change into these then."

"Awesome." He inhaled deeply just as my oven went off again. "Is that cookies I smell?"

"Yes!" Relief over the distraction of my awkwardness took over, and I hurried to the kitchen. Billy followed and exclaimed when he saw what I'd done in here.

"Wow! You did all this for tonight?"

I blushed as I took the last batch of cookies out of the oven and shut it off. "Yeah. I figured, go big or go home."

"I am honored, Lumen. Truly."

My heart soared. Maybe inviting a friend in wasn't so bad. This was a step in the right direction. Suddenly, Billy's phone started ringing and it brought me back from my thoughts. I lifted my bag.

"I'll go change."

Billy took out his phone and scrunched up his nose. "I'll take this real quick." He flashed the screen, and I saw the name NEVE pop up. My eyes widened, and I lost my breath.

I turned away quickly and ran to the bathroom.

No. It couldn't be the same woman. Could it? No.

I tried to force the intrusive thoughts as I changed into the matching PJs. I returned to the kitchen and found Billy admiring the gingerbread village I'd made.

"The detail on these houses is incredible, Lumen." He looked up from the gingerbread post office. "I mean, I knew you were cooking something up, you know, since I'm the one delivering your groceries, but I never imagined this! It's all edible?"

"Every piece! Although it might not taste good. Gingerbread houses aren't exactly made to be the best thing you have all Christmas. If you want something tasty, try one of these." I went to the counter and grabbed the tray of no bakes. He took one and took a bite.

"Oh, wow. This is delicious. I haven't had one of these in ages." He walked around the kitchen, continuing to admire the spread.

"I have cocoa too. I have lots of things to add to it. Marshmallows, syrups, whipped creams, even some adult adding. Just take your pick." I motioned with a sweep of my arm at the counter covered in sweet treats and mini bottles of liquor. Billy nodded appreciatively and then paused.

"Is this your house?" He pointed to a gingerbread house. I joined him at the island.

"It is. Was it the faulty Christmas lights that gave it away?" I laughed.

"The detail is uncanny." He shook his head. "Well, everything but these." He pointed to the thick, oversized candy canes sharpened to a point that surrounded the perimeter of the property. "I don't remember seeing these."

I tried to laugh it off, but failed miserably. "It's to keep the gingerbread bears at bay."

Billy grew quiet, and his happy face fell into one of sympathy.

"Lumen..."

I looked away. "I know, it's silly. It just... it made me feel better." We both knew that the candy cane spikes were a representation of the walls I built up around myself. "I know there's no gingerbread monsters here."

"There's no human ones here either," he whispered. I raised my head and saw Billy smiling softly at me. He reached forward, cupping my cheek. I jumped but forced myself to relax. "You're safe with me."

Politely, I pulled away and went to the cocoa station. "Let's get our treats and start our movie marathon." I picked up a tiny bottle of peppermint vodka and shook it excitedly, drawing his attention from my ominous gingerbread house.

"Now that's my favorite kind of ingredient for cocoa," Billy said. I offered him a large tray and took a matching one for myself. We filled them with cookies, cakes, cheese, crackers, brownies, and other treats, and then made our cocoa and went to the living room. I set a bunch of pillows on the floor and we plopped down, and I grabbed the remote, turning the TV up. We settled in just in time to see Ralphie's mother warning him that he'll shoot his eye out if he got the Red Ryder BB gun he wanted. We watched silently for about twenty minutes, until Billy turned to me, propping his head on his elbow.

"So, Lumen. I've seen you every day for the better part of this year, and I feel like I hardly know you."

My heart tightened, and I gulped. "What do you want to know?"

"Well... what's your favorite movie?"

All of this anxiety felt so absurd. Since the moment he got here, my alarms have been going up, only to be instantly dropped.

"Ooh, that's a hard one. Maybe *West Side Story?*"

"The new one?"

"Hardly." I rolled my eyes. "Rita Moreno supremacy. I was kind of a theater nerd growing up."

"Oh yeah? Tell me about it." He took a sip of his laced cocoa and offered me a mini bottle of the caramel-flavored vodka. I hadn't had alcohol in a long time. I'd only bought it for Billy. But...

I took it and emptied it into my hot cup. Bravely, I took a sip. And then another.

"Well, it started with *Grease*. I was obsessed with Rizzo. I used to put on my mom's shirts and stuff a pillow under it and pretend I was her."

We spent the rest of the movie getting to know each other. Billy had gone to school for computers, but dropped out to help take care of his aging grandparents. He had a DnD group he met with every Sunday night and played with for hours and hours. And his last relationship didn't exactly end great.

"She left me for a musician. I was too boring for her." He shrugged.

"Well, I think you're great," I said, my words running together. We'd both had more than one cup of adult cocoa. Mini liquor bottles were strewn across the floor. "And she thinks you're boring? Hell, I'm still a virgin."

"What?" Billy blinked rapidly.

Just then, we heard a sharp shattering sound come from the other room, and I leaped up. "Was that a window?" I swayed, trying to catch my balance.

"It was." Billy stood and snatched my wrist, clamping down on it so tight I gasped. "Merry Christmas, bitch."

RULE 5 - TOBIAS

FIGURE OUT WHAT YOUR FINAL GIRL NEEDS.

"Say cheese!" Neve squealed into my ear as she threw her arm over my shoulder. The four of us hunched over Lumen, bound, gagged, and blindfolded in a chair. Neve's camera went off with a loud click followed by a blinding flash. She rushed forward to reset the camera. "One more, for the Christmas card. Don't take off the masks."

We posed one more time as Lumen whimpered and sobbed in her seat. She'd been restrained at an impressively fast pace. Billy had her in a chair and was tying her up by the time we climbed through the window. Neve and Ruby finished with stuffing a rag in her mouth and tying a black silk scarf around her eyes.

"Perfect. Now, Billy, what did you find out?" Neve let us go, and we stepped away from the shaking girl.

"Uh, she's a theater nerd who's still a virgin?" Billy, the loser she'd convinced to join her game, scratched his head. "Do I gotta wear this? She already knows it's me." He lifted his matching mask and scowled at his girlfriend.

"Yes. It's for the aesthetic. Put it back on. Or I'll make

things so much worse for you all," she snapped. The blackmail she was holding over my head caused me to shut up and do as told.

"Where are you going?" Billy asked as I left the room.

"Let him explore, we need to focus here," Neve said.

I started through the house, looking at the walls. She'd decorated the walls with generic art from a big box store. Nothing looked personal. It was all decorated as if filling the house was an obligation, and none of it was Lumen.

Was that on purpose? Did she not want people to know who she was, even inside her own home?

I opened every door, peering inside, and seeing all the same. It was a staged home. I wondered then, if this was how she bought the house. My steps were slow as I pretended to be lost and unfamiliar with the layout. Neve had gotten a hold of the floor plan and told me to look at it. I had to hold back a laugh when she handed them to me. I'd seen those months ago, had even memorized them then. But I couldn't tell her that.

Neve had no clue how easy she was making things for me. She was convinced that she had me wrapped around her finger. She was wrong.

Saving Lumen's bedroom for last, I finally made it there and went inside, closing the door behind me. Flipping the light switch, I looked around and smiled.

There's my girl.

Her personality flooded the room. Red bedding, posters of shows on the walls. There was a desk stacked with notebooks in the corner, and clothes on the other side. I inhaled deeply, and my mind went right back to that afternoon last year.

Her perfume was imbedded in my memory. She'd smelled so good.

My cock hardened as I strode to her bed, imagining us on it. I'd thought about that day so much to the point of obsession. I'd jerked off to the pictures of us so many times. Now that I was so close to her, I needed to recreate them. And more.

I went to her desk and picked up a notebook. The pages were frayed, and as I flipped through, I saw that she'd written on every single page. I gazed up at the other notebooks. They were all written in, front to back. But it was her words that were unsettling.

7:00am alarm, shower, dress. Black shirt, jeans with rip in knee, matching yellow socks.

8:00am breakfast, one egg, one toast, coffee, cream, one peach.

10:00am Billy, mail. Orange long sleeves, jeans, brown boots. One step on porch, dropped packages, waved, left.

Her entire schedule was listed, day in day out. Every little detail about her interactions with people. Phone calls, Billy, literally everything was written down like a compulsion. But what stuck out was that she hadn't stepped out her front door in months. I set it down and returned to the living room.

"Find anything good?" Neve asked. "I was just explaining why we're here. How she ruined my life. How she's up here, living the rich life, pretending she didn't lie."

I stiffened. Neve was waving around a knife. Lumen was shaking, sobbing, and jumping at every word from Neve's mouth.

"You actually are here just in time for the fun to start. I've decided to be a gracious goddess. I can't let her die a virgin."

Billy lunged forward, grabbing Lumen's chest and ripping her shirt open. She screamed as her bra was revealed. I stepped forward and let a low growl escape my throat as I tore his hand away from her. He cocked his head.

"Ruby went back to the car to grab something to have fun with," Neve said, tugging both of us back. "She'd bought it for us later, but I think we'll just gift if to Lumen instead."

The front door burst open, sending another scream out from Lumen's gagged mouth. Ruby stormed in, stomping the snow off her boots as she came in with a box.

"Here." She thrust it at her girlfriend. I could only see her eyes, but I could tell she wasn't happy. "This was expensive."

Neve went to Ruby and placed her hand under her masked chin. "Darling, after we rob this bitch, money will be no issue."

Billy cleared his throat. I'd only known the two a week or so, but it was obvious that they both hated each other, but were either too scared or too in love to speak to Neve about sharing her. Ruby tore open the box, revealing a large, vibrating wand.

I stiffened. What was her plan?

"Hmm..." Neve walked around Lumen, tapping her chin. "Billy, can we cut a hole in the bottom of a chair?"

Billy ran to the kitchen and returned, dragging a chair in one hand and a large knife in the other. Setting it directly in front of Lumen, he stabbed the cushion and quickly carved a hole in it. Ruby handed him the vibrator, and he dropped it into the hole. The vibrating head rested on the top.

I clenched and unclenched my fists, trying to calm myself.

29

"Let's get her up," Neve ordered. "Tie her to the new chair."

I stepped forward, pushing Billy aside with a low growl. I crouched and took hold of Lumen's shaking legs. I leaned in and muttered, "Lumen, you're going to be okay. Just try to relax."

Her head shot up so fast.

"What are you saying to her?" Neve snapped.

"I told her if she didn't cooperate, she'd get cut," I lied, pulling out my knife and running it along Lumen's thigh. She whimpered as I untied her. She was instantly taken by Billy and Ruby, who forced her into the new chair, spreading her legs, and binding her tight. The vibrator rested directly under her pussy.

"This bad boy is so strong, I bet she'll piss everywhere in seconds. Where's the remote?"

"Give it to me," I ordered, putting my hand out.

"Nice try, I'm in control. Buckle up, bitch." Neve pressed the remote, and Lumen bolted forward, trying to escape the sensation.

"Just let it happen, Little Lumen." Neve cackled. "And know we're watching you. We'll know if you fake it."

I kneeled between Lumen's legs. She struggled against all of her restraints.

"It's okay," I muttered. I put my hand on her thigh, running up her leg. "Relax, enjoy it, Lumen."

She whimpered, but her fighting slowed. I reached up and removed her gag. She screamed, but she knew it was pointless, and stopped almost instantly, replacing it with moans and sobs.

"You monsters!" she gasped in between soft moans.

The three behind us laughed.

"Just come, and I'll stop," Neve said.

"Can you do that for me, Lumen?" I asked, keeping my voice low. She panted. She was fighting it. I ran my hand up the ripped shirt, across her breast, finding the hardened nub. I moved the bra, exposing her nipple. Pinched it and elicited a moan from her lips. "There we go, come on, baby, come for me."

My words seemed to be the trigger. At my order, she arched her back and cried out as she came. She rode the wand and then slumped forward. I cupped her face. "Good girl. You did so good."

"Shut it off." I turned back to Neve, but she shook her head, her eyes trained on Lumen. The mask covered the rest of her face, but I knew she was grinning ear to ear.

"No. Do it again."

RULE 6 - LUMEN

IT'S OKAY TO CRY.

My blood was on fire. My body was screaming in pain and oversensitivity.

"Please, turn it off," I begged. My humiliation was enough. Now they wanted to do it again? I didn't think my body could!

"Not until you come again. And again. I want your panties and pants soaked. I'll turn it off when the wand is wet. Ruby, check it."

I was still blindfolded, so I had to rely on my other senses. A figure came forward and put her hand between my legs.

"Dry as bone."

That bitch.

"Well, maybe she needs a little more help. Let's take her blindfold off," Neve ordered.

I was still so confused. How did she find me, and why? Someone undid the scarf, and I flinched as my eyes adjusted to the room. And then, my eyes connected with dazzling, familiar ones.

"Tobias."

His face was covered by a mask, but I'd know those eyes anywhere. I looked around at the others. They wore the same masks.

"Billy, why did you do this?"

"It must not be strong enough if you can talk." Neve pushed a remote in her hand and the machine under me grew stronger. I groaned. The pain was beginning to shift back to pleasure, but I couldn't do... that in front of everyone. Not now that I could see them too.

"There we go. Purr like a kitty. Let your little pussy drench the wand." She giggled. Tobias pressed his hand to my thigh again, and I looked back to him. He appeared to be trying to communicate with his eyes.

"Just let go," he whispered.

"I don't know if I can." Tears streamed down my face.

"You can. You can until I tell you to stop."

"Come on, Lumen, one more. Just one more for me," Tobias pleaded.

I took a deep breath and closed my eyes. I dug deep, remembering that afternoon a year ago. Tobias's hands, his scent, his lips....

"Oh!" I screamed as a second orgasm roared through my body. My blood was so hot, my heat so wet, I couldn't catch my breath. It was so warm in here...

"Hot? We can fix that. Hold on." Neve stopped the vibrator, and I slumped forward. Tobias reached for my face.

"You took that so well. You're beautiful, you know that, Lumen?"

Dizzy from the pleasure, I smiled lazily. But my smile quickly evaporated as I remembered the situation I was in. My home, my safety net, had been invaded. And I still didn't understand why.

I'd been so delirious with pleasure, I hadn't noticed Neve had left though the front door. I did however notice her reentrance. She was loud.

"Got it! Now, who wants to help poor, overheated Lumen?"

I swung my head to see her holding a long icicle. Panic slowly seeped into me as she walked further into the room. Tobias stood.

"What do you have that for?"

"Well, she's loosened up some. I'm sure she's nice and wet now. Let's get to the good part. Once she's had her innocence taken, we can take everything else and bounce."

"What are you taking?" I asked, my head swinging around the room.

"We know your family left you more than enough money to go around, Lumen. And, considering I have no money now, thanks to you testifying against Kane, I think it's fair that I be paid to help get me back on my feet," Neve said. "Now, who's going to do the honors?"

"Tobias." I looked to him. "Help me."

"He can't help you, sweetie. He's on our side. He's mad at you too."

"Why?" None of it made any sense.

"Untie her and get her undressed. What do you think, under the tree? I bet that will be a pretty place to lose your virginity." She stabbed the air with the icicle. "Hurry, before I have to go get another one."

"I'll do it." Billy leaped forward. He quickly untied my hands, and I slapped him as hard as I could. He fell back, but then came at me again. "Give me the fucking icicle. I'm using the sharp end."

"I don't want her dead yet," Neve snapped. "Hold her

arms so Ruby can finish untying her. Tobias, you're gonna do it."

"I'm not doing that," he said.

Relief flooded through me.

"Oh, I think you are," Neve shot back. The two had a stare off as Ruby untied me. Neve dropped the icicle on the ground and went outside as Billy made me stand, holding my arms behind my back. She returned, this time with a thicker, longer piece of ice. Was she implying that someone...

"Get her naked and hold her down."

"No!" Tobias and I yelled together.

"Do it, or I'm done playing games. I'll do what I warned you I'd do." Neve stormed over to Tobias and thrust the icicle into his hand. "Now fuck her with this."

I was too stunned and scared to do anything but stand there. Billy had his knife pressed to my back, reminding me that if I tried to run, he'd kill me now. Ruby stepped forward and tugged my pajama pants down. I wiggled to try to keep them, but she was rough and yanked them off completely, causing me to stumble. Billy caught me and reached around, ripping my shirt the rest of the way. He then took his knife and cut my bra from the back, exposing me completely to the room.

I put my head down in shame. More humiliation.

Twisting my arm, I was pushed forward to the Christmas tree and shoved to the ground. Neve and Ruby grabbed my legs and forced them open. Billy kept hold tight of my arms above my head.

"Don't touch her," Neve warned. "Save that for Tobias."

I looked up at Tobias. He hadn't moved a muscle. He was still standing there, mask on, with the icicle in his hand.

"One, two…" Neve threatened, and Tobias moved.

"Step back," he warned the girls, getting on his knees between my quivering legs.

No! All hope was dashed as he crawled closer.

"Tie her arms to something and then get away. I don't want you to touch her," Tobias ordered Billy. Ruby handed Billy the same rope I'd been restrained with before, and quickly I was tied to the trunk of the tree. If I tried to move, I'd take the tree down with me. Glass bulbs and lights hung on the tree. I'd be cut to hell.

That bastard.

"Well, get on with it." Neve crossed her arms impatiently. "Christmas is in an hour. I'd like to be celebrating at my hotel."

Tears streamed down my face as a draft ran through the room, causing my skin to pebble. My entire body was exposed to the room. All because of… what?

I lifted my head to look at Tobias. I gave him one last silent plea for him not to do this. What did she have over him to make him do her vile bidding?

"I'm going to go slow," Tobias said, and I let my body go slack. So this was it. I couldn't fight anymore.

Tobias's hands on my bare thighs sent shivers up my body. I closed my eyes and tried to go inside my mind.

"Good girl, pretend they aren't here," he whispered as he came closer. I jumped when his warm fingers found my sex and spread my lips.

"For being a virgin, she's so bare. I wondered if she planned on something tonight with you, Billy." Neve laughed.

A low growl vibrated against my sex, and I gasped as I felt something soft… lap my arousal. I squirmed as the good feelings warmed my body again. I forced myself deeper into myself, forgetting my audience.

Tobias ran his tongue against my sensitive flesh, causing me to moan and buck my hips. His hands reached up and teased my pebbled nipples.

"You're beautiful, Lumen. I've been waiting a year for this."

Me too. But I was too absorbed by his tongue to speak. Suddenly my body erupted a third time, and warmth gushed from my body. Tobias lapped it up, and then just as I was coming down, something freezing cold was placed against my entrance.

I stiffened.

"I don't want to do this," he whispered.

Then don't.

"Do it now, Tobias. This isn't meant to be fun," Neve spat.

I took a deep breath, braced myself, and bit my lip as slowly, Tobias inserted the ice into me. I cried out in pain. Not only was it freezing, but my body was tight and resistant to the invasion.

"Shhhh.... take it like a good girl," he ordered. His voice was like warm velvet. I attempted to relax as he pushed it further in, stretching and tearing me. Slowly, he pulled it out and then pushed it back in.

"Beautiful," he said as he began to fuck me with it. I groaned, and despite the shame, the fear, and anger, plea-sure reared its humiliating head once more. Tobias played with my clit as he thrust the melting ice into me.

"Deeper," I groaned. He hesitated, but I needed it, and bucked my hips, searching for a different release from the orgasms I'd had thus far. "Please."

He moved faster, pushed deeper. He stroked my clit

more, and one more thrust against something tender inside me sent me spiraling. I clenched my thighs together and screamed out for the fourth time tonight. I was mad, and scared, but also, so, so overjoyed to finally have my release.

Tobias removed the icicle and untied me. He pulled me into his arms, and I hugged him tightly. Why did I feel so good, having just been...

"Rape isn't supposed to feel good, for fuck's sake." Neve snarled. She came forward and tore me from Tobias's embrace. "Change of plans. If they won't hurt you. I will."

RULE 7 - TOBIAS

ONLY YOU CAN HURT YOUR FINAL GIRL.

I lurched forward when Neve yanked Lumen from my arms, but Billy grabbed me, shoving me back.

"Don't try anything funny." He slid his knife under my chin and pressed it to my throat. I forced myself not to jerk or twitch. This was like my day job. Working with animals, I had to make them feel in control. That I won't hurt them. In this case, however, I had no issue stabbing Billy the moment I catch him off guard.

Lumen scrambled to pick up her clothes. Her top was torn to shreds, but still she slid it back on, while Neve pointed her knife at her.

"Ruby, grab that." She motioned her head in my direction.

"Grab what? The icicle? Ew, no."

"Do it. Lumen is going to lick it clean." Neve smirked.

All eyes went to the tool. The side I'd put inside Lumen was covered in blood. I made eye contact with Ruby, and in a flash, we were both going for it. I managed to dive and get it first, and without another thought, I popped it into my mouth.

The cold ice was half melted and tasted like copper. It had fuzz from the carpet, but I pushed past all the contradicting tastes and textures and ran my tongue across it. As I sucked it clean, I locked eyes with Lumen. My lips and nose were still covered in her scent. My cock hardened as I sucked on the blood that I'd stolen from her. If it couldn't be my cock to have been gifted with it, I'd gladly take it this way.

Lumen's chin quivered as her brown eyes watered, making her even more gorgeous.

I finished and turned my attention to Neve and her cohorts, who were staring at me in disgust. I pulled the icicle from my mouth and tossed it at their feet. I stood, elbowing Billy back as I did.

Neve scowled. "What is this? Some kind of revolt? Can you not stand to see a damsel in distress? Jeez, you're weak, Tobias."

I bent and retrieved my mask. I needed to play this right. All three of them were holding knives. I slid it back over my face.

"This is no revolt. I think you underestimated my depravity." Slowly, I reached into my pocket, retrieving my switchblade. "I did fuck her with it, did I not?"

I couldn't look at Lumen as I said it, but in the corner of my eye, I saw her slinking slowly toward the front door. I could keep them talking.

Run, Lumen.

"Are you with us or not? Because if you're not, then we'll end this now." Neve stepped forward. "I bet Lumen isn't the only one who'd be interested in the video I have. Who should I call first? Your father or the police."

"What video?" Lumen's small voice drew the attention

to the edge of the room. Fuck, she'd been so close to the door.

Neve lifted her mask. "Oh, you want to see? It's the whole reason we're here, after all." She stomped over to Lumen and pulled out her phone.

"Lumen, get the fuck out of here," I ordered. "She's crazy. Don't listen to her."

"Oh, poor Lumen. It's not me who's crazy. It's your icicle lover over there who's the bad guy. Look." She tapped on her phone screen.

My insides twisted as Lumen's expression went from curiosity, to confusion, to shock, then finally, horror.

"What is..."

Billy stepped forward, his mask still on, but his eyes bright with glee. "Neve's old boyfriend didn't kill your family. He did." He swung his arm toward me, pointing his finger. He was close enough I lunged forward, grabbing his finger and bending it back until it cracked. He screamed and dropped to the ground.

"Asshole!" He pulled his mask off and tossed it on the ground.

I swung my foot out in the direction of his face. It collided with his nose in a loud crunch! He fell back with a loud scream. My fight with Billy distracted Neve enough to stop showing Lumen the video.

"Billy! Are you alright?" Neve ran to him.

"No, you dumb bitch! My nose is broken. Get me a towel or something."

"Dumb bitch?" Neve pulled back and stood. "Go get something from the kitchen. I'm not dumb, Billy." She spun back to us and shook her head. "That wasn't very team-like of you, Tobias."

"I'm not on anyone's team. I'm here for myself."

"What's that even mean?" Ruby sneered. "Neve, I want to leave. You had your fun. Let's get the money and go."

"There is no money," Lumen said. Our attention swung back to her as she trembled in the corner. "I don't know who told you that."

Billy swore and stood, rushing to the kitchen with his hand over his face. Ruby stepped forward, her fists clenched.

"What do you mean? Neve said—"

"Neve lied," I said. I knew there wasn't any money. I'd spent the better part of this year learning all about Lumen and her family. Her family was in debt when they died. I knew that, and so did Neve. Which was why I agreed to be blackmailed. I needed to see Neve's real intentions.

Ruby, Lumen, and I focused on Neve, waiting for her to expose the truth. The room was silent, other than the music playing in the background. The festive music contrasted with the tension in the room. Neve reached behind her, sliding her backpack off her shoulders.

"I did lie. I know you have no money. I also know that my life was ruined by you. Not only is the love of my life in jail for the rest of his life, but my career is ruined, and I was ostracized. I was run out of town for corrupting the community. I was turned into a monster, just because I was doing a viral trend."

She unzipped her backpack and carefully removed a slick, black handgun.

A small scream came from Lumen, while Ruby gasped.

"Babe, what are you doing?" Ruby raised her hands cautiously. "This wasn't part of the plan. Where did you get that?"

"It was Kane's. I took it when they were raiding his

house. I didn't want him getting more charges. It's not registered, so it's perfect for this." Neve raised it, pointing it at Lumen's chest. "Tell the room you lied."

"What?" Lumen raised her hands too. Her body trembled with fear. "What lie?"

"At the trial. You said Kane killed your family. He didn't."

"I didn't know that!" Lumen cried out, her gaze flickering to me for only a second before returning to the gun in Neve's hands. "I just found out about..."

"Your boy toy doing it? I don't believe that. I think you're both in cahoots, which is why I brought him here too. Tonight, you both die."

She turned quickly and pulled the trigger. Something behind me exploded and I dropped to the ground as the bang went off, deafening the room. I whipped my head around, looking for what she hit. The TV was black and had a giant hole in the middle. It was smoking and fizzling.

"Fuck," Neve yelled.

I leaped and tackled her, smacking the gun from her hand. It slid across the room. Ruby ran to it, picking it up.

"Help!" Neve screamed. "Don't let him rape me!"

I sat up in disgust. "I'm not going to rape you, you dumb bitch." I stared at her, and a sudden urge took over. I smirked and spat on her face.

"You bastard!" she screamed and threw me off her. She scrambled to grab for her backpack, but I scurried up as well. She was faster than me, running out the front door before I could catch my bearings. My ears were still ringing. I looked around the room, and found both Ruby and Lumen missing.

I couldn't spend too much time thinking about what to

do. I needed to cut off the head of the beast. I stormed out the front door into the cold.

A fucking gun? That was a coward's weapon. I braced myself for the temperature and jumped off the steps and followed the snowy footprints into the woods.

Neve was as good as dead.

RULE 8 - LUMEN

USE WHAT TOOLS YOU HAVE AVAILABLE.

I watched from the hallway closet as Neve ran out the front door. A moment later Tobias followed. I closed my eyes and tried to focus. My ears were still ringing from the gun shot, and my body hurt all over from the events of the night thus far. I wasn't sure what pain to focus on. My bruised ankles and wrists, the numerous cuts, or the sharp pain in my....

The memory of Tobias licking the evidence of my virginity off the icicle stirred things inside me. Shame mixed with arousal filled my body and soul in a way I wasn't sure how to handle. Tobias had made me come so much, my body craved more, despite seeing the video of him...

No. It couldn't be true. He couldn't have done that. Why would he run up to my unsuspecting sisters and parents and stab them repeatedly until...

It made no sense.

I inhaled deeply, trying to calm myself. I couldn't think about that right now. Right now, I needed to focus on surviving. I had to get everyone out of my house, and then,

I'd secure it and call for help. If my phone even worked. I had a feeling they'd taken care of that.

I rummaged on the floor and found my Carhart boots. I hadn't worn shoes in months. There was no need when you didn't leave the house. I quietly slid them on, sans socks. I laced them, and stood, taking a few test steps. The weight was uncomfortable, and I felt a little silly, but... just in case.

Cautiously, I opened the closet door and peered out. The hallway was silent, except the music from the kitchen. Miley Cyrus was singing about sleigh rides as I crept through my destroyed house, examining the damage. My TV was sparking from the bullet hole. The chair Billy had turned into my sexual torture device lay on its side, surrounded by broken cups, spilled cocoa, and shattered ornaments. I paused at the bare spot by the tree. There was a wet spot, where the icicle that had taken my virginity had finally melted.

My heart stuttered at the memory of Tobias's lips and hands on my tender flesh. He'd made the best out of the humiliating, horrific situation.

He also murdered my entire family.

My mind was reeling with the whiplash of everything that had happened this evening. Billy swearing from the kitchen pulled my attention from the tree. I went inside and found him leaning against the counter with a kitchen towel to his nose.

"Why are you doing this?" I asked.

"I could ask the same to you." He waved his hand around the full spread of treats. The cookies, brownies, and gingerbread house completely untouched of tonight's atrocities. The entire kitchen, in fact, felt like it was in a different world. The music still played loudly, and it smelled of vanilla and... Christmas.

"Why did you do all this for me? You were more than happy to spread your legs for Tobias. Feels dumb to think you liked me now."

I gulped.

"I wanted to like you."

"But you didn't?"

No.

"Have you ever liked anyone? Or have you always been a frigid bitch?"

I flinched. I'd been in love once. Engaged to be married, even. And then he dumped me for a Mariah Carey impersonator. I thought that would be the worst thing to ever happen to me. What I'd give to be that naive again. I steeled my nerves and turned to Billy.

"Don't go all incel on me, Billy. Just because I didn't want to fuck you, doesn't mean I didn't want to at all."

He tossed the towel on the counter with a growl. "That's obvious. You opened up so wide for him to shove that icicle up your pussy. If it wasn't for all the blood, I'd be certain you were a camera slut."

I stared at his swollen face. His nose was bent all to hell, and his eyes were a deep purple. He snickered.

"Not gonna lie, though. I almost came in my shorts, watching you wiggle in that chair. Neve was getting jealous, but fuck her." He kicked off the lower cabinets and started toward me. "It's my turn." His hands went to his pants.

Fear bolted through my spine, and I stepped back.

"Don't come near me, you bastard." I looked around the kitchen, searching for something to arm myself. The knife holder had been completely emptied. I'd known that though. I'd see them scattered in my living room amid the rest of the destruction.

"Why not? You afraid of trying a real cock? I bet I'm bigger than him. Better too. He gives small dick energy. He didn't even have the balls to tell you himself what he did to your parents."

My eyes went to his groin, where he'd slid his penis out. I grimaced and looked away. The first penis I'd ever seen, and it was a guy with the intent of raping me.

What was the line, though?

Tobias had done the same. I'd pleaded for him not to do it, and he still forced the icicle inside me. He tore me, hurt me, made me bleed. I sobbed, begged, and... wanted more.

No. I shook the mixed thoughts from my mind. I didn't want to feel good about what Tobias had done. He was no better than Billy. He held his stiff cock while he advanced on me.

"Don't touch me," I warned, stepping around the island.

"Or what? You'll hurt me with your cookies? Lumen, you're a fucking joke. Everyone in town makes fun of you. That's why I'm the one to deliver your stuff. Everyone else refuses to give in to your delusions. If it weren't for me, you would have starved months ago. That feels like it deserves a little something. Maybe a little kiss from you? What do you say, princess? Blow me, and I'll let you go."

I gagged at the idea. I didn't even do that with Ben when we were engaged. There was no way my first time was going to be for Billy.

I grabbed a tray of cookies and dropped the treats on the floor. I swung the silver tray in his direction. "Don't come near me. I'll knock you out."

"And then what? Toss me out? I'll just come back. And if I don't, what will you do? Who will bring you your mail or deliver food? You're too chicken-shit to step out onto the porch. You need me, Lumen. Just give me what I want, and all of this can go away. I'll tell Neve to back off. I'll send Ruby packing. She annoys me anyway. Always trying to steal Neve from me. I'll get them both off your back, and then we can go back to how things were. I keep you safe, alive, and in return..."

He ducked as I swung the plate again. He abandoned his cock to grab for me, but I stepped back. He lunged for me and caught my arm, twisting it behind my back. He took my other hand and did the same, leaving me defenseless.

"Being difficult is what has gotten you this deep in trouble. If you just let things happen as they should have, none of this would have happened."

He moved behind me, and I tried to kick him away as he pressed his groin against me. I pressed my lips together tight and fought back tears as I tried to fight against what he was about to do. Somehow, this felt so much worse than what Tobias had done. This was the ultimate violation.

I couldn't go down without a fight.

I looked around for something to use against him. And then... I saw it. The gingerbread house, directly in front of me.

"Just let it happen, Lumen. This is just for me, so it'll go quick," Billy muttered into my ear, triggering me to move. I spun out of his grip and snatched his hair. With my other hand, I grabbed for the house and pulled it to the edge of the counter. Using all the strength I could muster, I shoved his head down into the house.

Billy screamed as his head collided with the sharpened candy canes. He threw his body back, and I collapsed to the floor and stared in horror as he lifted his head up. The house, smashed, lay abandoned on the counter, but the candy canes came up with him. Two of them were plunged deep into his eyes. They'd gone so deep, only the tips were visible. He stood, screamed one last time, and then dropped to the ground.

I stood, my entire body shaking as I walked over to his twitching body. Did I... was he...

I stared at him with candy canes where his eyes used to be, with his cock hanging out of his pants. Any sympathy I'd had momentarily was gone in an instant. I steeled myself and started out of the room.

I did. He was.

Good.

Now. To find the others.

RULE 9 - TOBIAS

SHOOT YOUR SHOT.

The bloody scream rang out from the house. I froze and turned back. It wasn't Lumen's. It was a man's scream. I weighed my options. Should I continue to hunt Neve, or should I return and make sure Lumen was okay?

I huffed, realizing how ridiculous the question was. I abandoned my search for the goth bitch with the trigger finger and returned to the house. I stepped inside, the Christmas music assaulting my ears. I listened for more screams, but heard nothing but Kelly Clarkson singing about being wrapped up in red.

I crept into the house, my boots crunching on pieces of wood, baked goods, and ornaments that had fallen and rolled away from the tree. I turned into the kitchen.

"Lumen?"

I looked around, and saw a mess. The island of treats had been destroyed. Cookies were strewn all over the counter. Plates had been shattered and sprinkles littered the floor. There had been a fight; I could see footprints in the smashed treats. I followed them around the island and then stopped short.

Billy's body lay splayed out on the floor. I crouched down to examine just exactly what happened. His dick was hanging out of his open pants, and his eyes... I leaned closer, flicking the small pieces still showing from the wounds. Candy canes.

Jesus Christ.

I stood, looking at the scene as a whole. He deserved whatever went down.

That's my girl.

I left the kitchen and started searching the rest of the house.

"Ruby? Lumen?" I called, opening every door and turning on every light. Ruby fled when the gun went off. I wouldn't be surprised if she'd taken the car.

I didn't blame her.

Soft sobbing sent me to Lumen's room. I moved softly, to not alert her. The lights were off, and as I opened the door, it creaked loudly. Shit.

"Come out, come out, wherever you are, Lumen." I went to the closet, whipping it open. I looked down and saw her looking back up at me, tears streaming from her face.

"You did that to Billy, and now you're here hiding? Seems a little contradictive." I pulled her up and dragged her from the closet. She dug her boots into the floor, but my strength outweighed hers.

"There's someone on the roof!" she hissed.

"What?" I asked and suddenly a bang rang out just outside the door. I whipped the door open and saw a smoking hole in the floor. I looked up to see where it had come from.

"Sssh, she'll hear us!" Lumen whispered. I crept back in

the room as quietly as I could. I sat down on her bed and looked at her. We were trapped in here.

"He was going to rape me," she said, joining me on the bed. "I was defending myself."

"And what exactly did I do?"

She glared. My body reacted to her anger; my cock hardening. She was gorgeous when she was angry. She stood, and I joined her. We were both careful to keep our voices down and our steps light.

"You did what you were told. Billy didn't have someone with a gun telling him to do it."

"And what if I told you I didn't either?"

"What are you saying?"

"I'm saying, what if it was all an act. To get you to trust me." I wrapped my arms around her and pressed her to me. She looked into my eyes, searching for the lie.

"You killed my family," she whispered.

"I did."

"Why?"

My mouth suddenly went dry. It hit me then that she wasn't fighting my embrace. She didn't seem angry, she was... sad. I opened my mouth but nothing came out.

I held her closer as she silently cried, but then a loud sob erupted from her, and we both jumped as another bang came, this time only feet from us.

"Don't make a sound."

Her eyes turned hard and she tugged out of my arms. She went to the bedroom door and slammed it. Ruby shot down again, missing her. I yanked her back and smacked my hand over her mouth to stop her from screaming. I pressed my body to hers.

"You want to know why I slaughtered your entire family? Fuck me for it." My cock strained against my jeans. I spun her around to look her in the eyes. They were frightened, which only made me want her more. I leaned closer to her, so that I could whisper in her ear. "Ruby is up there, right now, waiting for you to make a sound. How many bullets do you think she has left?"

I knew the answer, but did she?

I ran my hand along the side of her breast, her ripped pajama top that covered almost nothing now that her bra had been cut off.

"You didn't have a choice before, with everyone watching. But now you do. You have something I want. And I have something you want."

"What is it exactly you want?" she whispered.

"You to *choose* me."

She blinked. We stared at each other for a long moment and then she nodded. I took that as a yes, and slowly I stepped back and reached for her torn shirt, pulling it over her head and tossing it aside. I did the same with mine, and then my boots and pants. She stared at me, completely bare to her, and then undressed herself as well. I took her to the bed. It squeaked with the weight of us, and Ruby shot again.

My ears were ringing. Lumen grimaced, but I put my finger on her lips to silence her. She nodded.

I reached for her and urged her to sit on my lap. She was shaking like one of my dogs. I tried to calm her as she straddled my lap. I stroked my cock and directed her with my hands. I fingered her pussy, and found her already soaked. I took her arousal and coated my cock with it before setting it against her entrance. I leaned forward and whispered in her ear, "Let's make her unload this clip."

She looked confused and then I shoved her down, my cock pushing into her. She cried out in pain, and Ruby shot down at us. Lumen bit down on her lips and stared into my eyes. Tears filled the corners of her eyes as she took every inch of me. I forced the groan threatening to come from my throat down. Her walls clenched my cock in a wet, hot, delicious tightness that made my balls ache.

I gripped her and stood, walking to her desk. I sat her bare ass on it and began to thrust.

"Oh god," she gasped. Ruby shot again. The bed behind us exploded. I grinned and lifted her again. I pulled the chair out a few feet and sat, with her on top.

I urged her hips up, and then back down.

"Good girl, Lumen," I praised, eliciting two more bullets from Ruby. She was shit at taking direction. She'd shot down from all the way across the room.

I lifted Lumen up again and back down until she figured out the rhythm I wanted. She squirmed on my cock like a baby fowl, learning to use its legs. It was hot, and I had to focus on not coming. I brought my head down to take a nipple into my mouth. She was gorgeous with her head thrown back as she ground her clit against my body.

I'd waited almost a full year for this. I'd dreamed of our bodies, naked and pressed against each other's almost daily. I'd felt something that day of the photoshoot. Something more than just lust. I'd felt a connection, and I'd spent a year preparing for it. She'd never called me, but I knew that eventually, we'd find our way back to each other.

And now, here we were. Her pussy clenching my cock for dear life, her mouth panting my name. Her clit pleading for me to play with it. I rubbed the pad of my thumb over her sensitive nub, and she gasped.

"Sssh..." I reminded her. "Don't let Ruby hear you. She'll shoot." I laughed.

Lumen put her arms over my shoulder and began to bounce and grind harder.

"Good girl, get yours, so I can fill you with mine," I growled into her ear. She nodded and ground her pussy harder down on me. A moment later, she cried out and her pussy began pulsing as she unraveled in my arms. Her cry was loud. Ruby's footsteps were just as loud down here as she ran to us. I stood quickly and threw Lumen onto the already shot through bed.

Ruby shot two more times behind us as I plunged my cock into Lumen's soaked pussy. How many did she have left?

"Why did you do it?" Lumen asked, her back arching as I fucked her.

"What?" I'd completely forgotten about everything. I must have been too loud because a second later another bullet was shot only feet away from us.

"Why did you kill my family?"

I licked my lips and the words refused to take shape.

How could I tell her the truth?

"Lumen, I—" My orgasm came on without warning. My balls tightened, and I exploded inside her. I pumped my cum into her, my mind reeling with the desire to fill her with my seed. No matter what happened tonight, she was mine now.

My groan sent one more bullet ringing just outside the door. I pulled out of her and stared at her. She was fighting back tears.

"You're a monster," she said.

Retrieving our clothes, I got dressed quickly and smirked. "Am I? Because how I see it, I keep saving your life." I pointed to the ceiling, where Ruby was pacing the roof. "She's out of bullets."

RULE 10 - LUMEN
DON'T BE SHOCKED WHEN THINGS GO RIGHT SOMETIMES.

"What am I supposed to do?" I slid my boots on and started after Tobias.

"Get Ruby. I'm going to deal with Neve." He reached into his back pocket, pulling out a switchblade. He opened and slammed the front door just as I reached him. I touched the handle, turned, and froze. I couldn't pull it open. I turned and leaned against the door, slowly sinking down.

For the first time since I moved in, I didn't feel safe here. I felt... trapped. What was I supposed to do? A loud *thunk* came from my guest room. I wiped my tears and stood quickly. A moment later, Ruby appeared, her mask back on. She turned her head slightly, trying to intimidate me.

"How is someone like you so hard to kill?" She took a step closer, and I pressed my back to the door, reaching behind me for the door handle. My heart pounded in my ears as I tried to turn the handle. I couldn't. I closed my eyes again, but it was too late. The screams from the mall were deafening me.

You can't leave! It's not safe!

Beads of sweat dripped down my chest as I tried to shove down the dark fears. Ruby inched forward, knowing I was cornered and had nowhere to go. Finally, I spun around and gripped the handle. I pulled the door open, but froze. It was dark outside past the porch. I couldn't go out there. I'd be sucked into the darkness and at the mercy of whatever was out there.

Neve, Tobias, someone worse.

"What are you going to do, Lumen?" Ruby mocked.

I lifted my foot but placed it right back down. I couldn't. I stepped back to shut the door, but Ruby was close and I felt her hands on me right before she shoved me outside.

I fell to the porch, my hands stinging instantly from catching myself on the half-melted snow. She shut the door, following me out.

"Look at you, taking healthy steps. How long has it been since you've been this far out of your house?"

Terror squeezed my heart as I rushed to the door, only to find it locked.

"Not this time." Ruby clicked her tongue. "I saw what you did to Billy. You're next if you don't fight for it." She grabbed my hair and yanked me from the door. I fell to the porch again and screamed in anguish. She stood over me with her stupid mask. Without another thought, I lifted my legs and kicked her in the gut, sending her across the porch.

"You bitch!" she screamed as she scrambled up. I joined her. She had the advantage. Not only was she not terrified of every little thing, she was wearing full winter gear. All I had was the thin, torn pajamas and my boots. I was drenched in the slush that was passing for snow on my porch. Everything was half melted.

I looked around. All around, the various Christmas

decorations were placed around the platform haphazardly. Billy had set up everything for me to see through the windows. I needed back inside. I couldn't fight her out here. She had the advantage. I was searching for a window to break when Ruby let out a scream, and I turned just in time to see her running at me with a large plastic reindeer over her head.

I ducked just as she reached me and swung down. I rolled and picked up a large, plastic candy cane. I smacked her calves with it and rolled again out of her reach. She continued her attack, swinging the giant decoration at me, landing a few hits. After realizing it didn't do much damage, she abandoned it and picked up a glass ornament. She threw back her mask.

"Catch," she ordered as she pitched the beach-ball sized ornament at me. I dropped to the ground and covered my head as it hit my back and shattered into a million pieces. Shards of glass stung my back through my clothes. I quickly stood and shook off the glass, then looked around for something to fight her off.

There was nothing but plastic animals and glass bulbs. Unless I wanted to step off the porch... I crept slowly to the stairs, but stopped short. I... I couldn't.

"You little chicken shit," Ruby mocked. "Neve told us about you. How even before the photoshoot, you were a mousy little thing. How your sisters had to sign you up because you were so scared of your shadow, they thought you'd never leave their house. Looks like they were right."

Flashes of my sisters went through my mind. They'd only wanted what was best for me, taking us to the mall that day. And what did it get them? Murdered. Murdered by Tobias. I spun around.

"Why did Tobias kill my family?" I blurted. "Do you know?"

"Why would I know?" Ruby laughed. "If I had it my way, we would have offed him before we did you. Neve has a soft spot for what he does and didn't want to leave all his animal rescues to starve."

I cocked my head.

"He saves dogs from dire situations, because of course he does." She rolled her eyes. I realized then that if I kept her talking, I could get her to relax, and I could make a run for it.

"What does that mean?" I inched away from the steps, keeping my eye on the closest window. It was locked, but I could break it and climb in.

"He's ridiculously hot, charming, and has a job that would send any woman to her knees. Even Neve wants him. That's why we're here, you know."

I shook my head, genuinely confused. Ruby kept going.

"Neve never loved Billy. She's been obsessed with Tobias since the photoshoot. She looks at your photos all the time. She tried to contact him. She asked his dad for his number, but his dad said he was taken. Some girl from a photoshoot had his heart. Neve doesn't want your money. She wants your man."

I blinked. My man?

"I haven't seen Tobias since that day."

Ruby snickered. "It doesn't matter. Once Neve wants something, she'll do whatever it takes to get it. Look at us." She motioned to the house and then at herself. "Billy's dead, and she told me to not bother coming back to her unless you're dead."

"Then why bother? She's not good for you."

"Love does crazy things. Sorry, you have to die." Her sad

face turned determined. She jumped, hooking her hands on the gutter.

What was she doing? I wondered, but then watched as she yanked the lights down.

"Oh—" I started to warn her, but then stopped. She literally just told me I had to die. Why would I help her? I stood back and let her pull down the old, faulty lights.

"Ouch," she winced as she got shocked.

Just like Billy had.

Back on the porch, she turned and smiled wickedly. "I'm going to decorate you like a tree. Tobias is going to come back to the house to see you strangled with the lights around your neck."

My eyes went to the porch, where the snow was melted. I stepped back, and she stepped forward.

The electric lights were snapping and popping and let off a loud hum as she dragged more of them down. I continued to walk backward, watching her footsteps carefully. She stopped moving when she saw what I was watching.

"You think I'm stupid? These lights are old. I'm not getting electro—"

I ran forward with my hands out and shoved her back, like she'd done to me to get me outside. She flew back into the puddle behind her, still holding tight to the faulty lights.

The lights let out a loud electric hum as her body lit up and then went stiff.

The bottom of my boots are rubber. They didn't conduct electricity. I stared at her limp body. Her mouth was frozen in shock, her eyes wide and gone. It all happened so fast, I wasn't sure how to feel. I felt... alive.

I was still alive.

I turned and looked around. I'd made it to the porch for the first time in months. And I survived. A slow smile slid over my face.

I survived.

I left my house and wasn't immediately murdered.

Ruby was. So was Billy.

But I was alive.

I inhaled the cold, fresh air as if it were the first time.

I was alive.

Good.

Now, for the last one.

Neve.

RULE 11 - LUMEN
RUN. BITCH. RUN.

Taking a deep breath, I stepped onto the stairs. I paused, then took another. Then one more, and soon, I was on the ground. The crunch of the snow under my boots was foreign, scary, and yet, invigorating. I looked back at the house. I could have gone back inside, hidden, looked for a phone or tried my internet, but I didn't.

I'm moving forward.

I inhaled again, steeled myself, and took a step toward the pitch-black trees.

Every step away from the house was like a tether being stretched. In an instant, I could be yanked back, and a part of me wanted to return to the house and hide. Another part of me knew that I needed to do this. I needed to find Tobias.

He told his dad I had his heart.

A man I'd known for an afternoon. A man who'd taken my virginity by force with an icicle but still tried to make it feel good. A man who later fucked me loudly to get an intruder to shoot off all their bullets. A man who...

I stopped short when I heard voices.

"You can't let her live," Neve said from somewhere in the darkness. "You saw her face when she saw the video. She'll tell the police. You'll go to prison, and all those animals will starve to death. Let's just end things now and get out of here."

My stomach twisted. Was she talking to Tobias?

I moved closer toward her voice. Someone was replying, but the voice was too low to identify. I was sure I could get close when I stepped on a twig and it snapped loudly under my boot.

"What was that?" Neve asked. Suddenly she ran out from behind a tree about ten feet ahead of me. She pointed dramatically and snarled, "You. How did you get out?"

"I-I can leave whenever." I didn't believe it for a second, but I tried to be strong.

"Yeah?" She put her hand on her hip. "And what is going to happen if you leave? Where are you planning on going? I bet I can get you back to that house in a flash and once you're there, you won't ever leave again." She reached for her backpack again.

She was right. If I ran back inside, I'd never go back out. I'd live the rest of my life hidden away. And if no one brought me food, then my fears truly would be the death of me. I'd be found in a closet, having starved to death and scared to turn on the lights.

Neve dug into the bag and pulled out a large knife, unsheathing it.

"I can't miss with this one. You better run, Lumen. Because when I catch you, I'm going to carve pretty little designs into your flesh. Tobias won't be able to recognize you."

I bolted to the right, heading further into the darkness.

While my eyes had adjusted to the lack of light, I was still tripping on everything.

"You might want to be quiet. Your little screams are going to lead me right to you."

I pressed my lips tightly together and focused on moving slower and stepping on snow, but the first patch I caught turned out to be slush and I slipped and fell face-first. My head hit the cold, ground hard, and I saw stars. I struggled to my feet and tried to wipe the snow and mud off.

"Gotcha!" Neve shouted as she popped from behind a tree and swung her knife. I scurried back and ran in the other direction.

"You only saw the video without sound. You should hear it with the volume turned up. Your parents' screams are horrific. But that didn't stop Tobias. He was smiling as he massacred your family. Is that the man you want? You should just give up. He wasn't meant for someone like you."

She taunted me as she chased me through the woods. While I was still confused about my feelings, I knew jealousy when I felt it.

She thought she was meant to be with Tobias?

Over my dead body.

I wasn't going to let that happen. I clenched my fists and turned. She came upon me a moment later and I swung my fist. It collided with her cheek, sending her reeling back.

"You bitch!" she screamed as she fell down. I lunged for her, straddling her middle. I grabbed her arms and held her to the ground. The knife was in her right hand. I squeezed her wrist to drop it.

"You think Tobias will want you after this? You're delusional." I snickered. She kicked her legs up, trying to hit me. I laughed and leaned down to whisper. "Tobias is mine."

Her eyes went wide and suddenly she regained her strength. She yanked her arm out of my grip and swung at me. I screamed as the knife sunk into my shoulder blade.

I fell back, the knife still in place. Neve scurried up, kicking me to roll over. She gripped the knife and tore it from my flesh, causing white, hot, excruciating pain to shoot through me.

"Say that again and I'll end things right here."

I trembled as I rocked, trying to breathe through the pain.

"But I'm not entirely ready for this to be over. I want to drag this out. We've waited a full year, you know. I want Tobias to see the life go out of your eyes as he and I make love."

I rolled over and managed to get on all fours. My body was screaming for me to lie back down, but I refused to give up. Neve kicked my ribs, sending me to the ground again.

"Get up and start running. I'll give you a head start."

I struggled to my feet and glared at her.

"Tobias would never touch you."

She laughed. "Really? Because he already has. We've been together this whole time. Why do you think he was so quick to do what I ordered? Tobias was never yours. You might want to move before I stab you again."

We didn't speak for a moment, so I turned and limped away. I couldn't run like before. My back was on fire, and I could hardly breathe. The further I got, the easier it became. I was able to walk slowly.

Tobias and Neve? I didn't want to think about that. He couldn't have done what he did with me and also do it with her.

But he also did kill my family.

I saw the video, my parents, then my sisters. He spared no one, and like Neve said, he'd been smiling the entire time. Why did he do it? And why was I conflicted over it?

I should hate him for what he did, but... I wasn't sure I could.

"Lumen..." His voice in the darkness startled me. I spun around and glared.

"Go away!" I demanded, even though I didn't want him too. I wanted to ask for his help. I was freezing, my fingers and toes numb. My clothes and face were covered in wet snow and mud, and I had a gaping wound in my back.

"Lumen." Tobias stepped out from the trees. My heart squeezed with yearning to run into his arms, but instead I stepped back.

"Don't come near me. You've been on her side this whole time, haven't you?"

"What are you talking about? Lumen, watch—"

"Watch what? That video of you stabbing my mom and dad and then my sisters to death? I don't need to see it again. Once was enough. You're a sick bastard."

His face fell, shattering my resolve. He was so hand-some, and his hands had been so kind to me. Was this the same man from that video? I continued backing up, until I stumbled on something slick.

I turned but the movement made me fall completely, and I realized I was on ice. I'd made it to the lake.

Oh no.

My body shook as I tried to scoot carefully back to land. I'd never been on ice like this? Could it hold my weight?

"Jesus Christ," Tobias snarled and stomped out of the trees. I pivoted, deciding the ice was safer, but I was too slow, and a second later Tobias's hand was on my pajama shirt, yanking me back to land. I screamed as pain shot through my shoulder. It was blinding hot and I couldn't breathe for a moment.

My body was going through shock, hot from the stab wound, yet trembling from the cold. I feared it was also from being this close to Tobias again. My body revolted against my mind. His warm breath on my neck sent delicious shivers down my body straight to my core. After all I'd experienced tonight, I still craved more. I hated him, and yet... needed him. I groaned and pushed my ass against his groin. He was hard.

He wanted me too.

"There's no escaping, Lumen. You're going to finally fucking listen, and then you're going to be mine."

RULE 12 - LUMEN
DRESS FOR THE WEATHER

"Let me go!" I struggled against Tobias's hold. He had one hand wrapped around my throat, and the other was sliding down my torso, heading to my groin. His fingers slid under the band of my pajamas and went down to my heat. Expertly, he parted my lips and leaned into me.

"Are you wet from before, or did this just happen?"

"You bastard!" I snarled as he pushed a finger inside me and swirled my wetness around my clit, eliciting a moan from my throat. I should be sore, worn out, and too sensitive, but I wasn't. I needed more.

Suddenly, he removed his hands and pushed me forward. I was unprepared and threw my hands out in front of me to catch myself, landing on all fours on the freezing cold ice. My shoulders were pushed back and I bit my lip, trying to not collapse from the pain. My wound was wide open and bleeding, causing silent tears to fall down my face onto the ice.

A second later, Tobias was directly behind me, his hand placed firmly on my lower back. "What are you doing?" I tried to scurry further onto the ice, but he grabbed my top and held me in place. "It's cold, please!"

"No. You're going to fucking see why I did what I did." Tobias leaned over me, pressing his warm body to my shivering one. His hand went around and a cell phone was placed on the ice, directly under my head. My stomach tightened as I saw the familiar video. It was the same one Neve had shown me.

"I don't want to watch this again, please, let me go. I'm going to get frostbite!" I pleaded with him, but I was ignored. Instead, he pushed Play and then turned up the volume.

"Neve didn't show you the full video, with audio."

Realizing he wasn't going to let me go, I shifted my hands, tugging down the shirt to try to cover my exposed skin, and stared down at the screen showing my family's last moments.

"She'll be out soon," Tauren said. "The photo session was for two hours."

My chin trembled, hearing her voice for the first time since her death. Poor Tauren.

"We did what you asked. Gave her one last good day," Shy said.

"Good. And the life insurance policy is good to go. Twenty million total," Dad boasted.

Life insurance? What was he talking about.

"I hate this. Do we have to kill her?" Shy pouted, stomping her foot. "I've heard of others not killing people to do it. Some just stab themselves. This streamer I watch did it—"

"No." Dad shut her down. "Your mother and I are too old to do the ritual that way. We'll die in the process. The

Reanimator requires younger blood. We discussed this already. Lumen is the way to go."

"It just sucks that it has to be her," Tauren added. "Can't we just kill a member of the unhoused?"

"The unhoused? No, Tauren, sweetie." Dad went to her, putting his hands on my older sister. "We've spent a full year planning this. We gave your sister one last good day. She's had food she loves, presents, and something fun that you picked out for her. Now we're going to take her home and do what has to be done."

What was my dad saying? He'd planned on killing me?

"Keep watching, Lumen," Tobias said, a hint of warning in his voice. It was then that I noticed his groin was pressed against my ass, his hands on my hips. They were slowly caressing my sides. "I want you to see exactly what happened that afternoon."

I didn't, but I had to know. I sniffled, wiped my tears, and kept watching.

"Okay, okay. You're right, Daddy. We did plan this for so long. We can't go back now."

Tobias's hands explored my body lazily. I found myself arching my back and pushing back against him.

"Keep watching," he reminded me as my family sat down on a bench and discussed methods of killing me. Slowly, he pulled my pajama pants down to my thighs and parted my legs. I didn't fight him, instead, I raised my ass to him. A moment later, I heard the tinkling of his belt being undone, and soon his cock head was at my entrance.

"You're so cold," he muttered.

"I know," I said, my teeth chattering.

"Watch. Those are the real bastards, not me." Slowly, Tobias pushed inside me, causing me to gasp at the invasion. It was so tight, it hurt. "Ssshhh..." he tried to soothe me.

"Tobias, you won't fit!"

"Yes, I will. Are you doing as told?"

I looked down just as Tobias appeared from around the corner.

"Were you talking about Lumen?" he demanded in the video to my parents.

Dad stood first, then Mom and my sisters.

"Who are you?" Dad demanded. "Get out of here."

"You're going to kill her?" Tobias asked, and Dad chuckled.

"You're too young to understand, kid. Get out of here before I call security or something. You don't know who you're talking to."

As I focused on the video, Tobias pulled slowly out of me, and then pushed back in. I was gasping, and wincing, but... it felt good. He was pushing against something inside of me that needed pushed.

"Tobias," I moaned, pressing my aching pussy into him. He growled and began thrusting at a more even pace. My orgasm was building at an alarming rate.

"Lumen," he growled.

I looked down again, just in time to see Tobias pulling his switchblade from his pocket.

"I can't allow you to do that."

Dad put his hands up and Mom and my sisters hid behind him.

"You don't know what you're doing, son. They'll find you. You'll go to prison."

Tobias lunged, plunging the knife deep into my father's chest. Dad dropped instantly, and Tobias moved to Mom, slashing her stomach and then her neck. Shy and Tauren tried to run, but he quickly caught them, dragged them back, and ended their lives quick. All the while I was watching my family be massacred, the man who had done it was plunging his cock deep inside me.

I closed my eyes and focused on how good it felt. Tobias reached around and cupped my breasts, pinching my rigid nipples.

"Do you understand now why I did what I did? I had to save you, Lumen. They didn't love you, but I did. I still do. You were mine then, and you're mine now. I'll do anything for you."

He spoke as he thrust, each new sentence sending me into more and more delirious pleasure.

"I can't live without you. That's why I came. We're getting out of here, and you're coming with me."

"Where?" I asked, not really caring, but I was curious. At this point, my body was so boiling and on the edge of ultimate orgasm, I would agree to just about anything right now.

"You'll see," he said. "I know you're close. Come on, be a good girl, Lumen, and drench my cock. Come, baby."

"Harder," I panted. He listened, and within three hard thrusts, I was shoved over the edge and I screamed as my body erupted and shook as my orgasm flooded my system with pleasure.

Tobias moved slow, allowing me to come down, and then he returned to his feverish pace until he suddenly stiffened and groaned loudly, his own release coming. He pumped himself into my wanting flesh. He removed himself from me and pulled my pants up, grabbing his cell phone.

"Do you understand now? I'd just found you, I wasn't going to let them take you from me."

I threw my arms around him. "And now they never will."

While it wasn't conventional, I was happy we'd found each other again. He wasn't my villain; he was my hero. And he was right, I was his now. I wanted that just as much as he did.

"They might not have taken you, but that just means I'll have to finish the job."

We stiffened and looked to the shore, where Neve walked out from the trees, holding another gun.

"Sorry, you don't get a Merry Christmas, after all."

RULE 13 - TOBIAS

KEEP YOUR EYES ON YOUR FINAL GOAL, TO GET YOUR FINAL GIRL.

"Neve, where did you get that?" I stared at the weapon in her hand. I raised my hands and slowly stepped off the ice. My feet slipped on the spots in which Lumen and I had been resting our hands and knees on, having melted the ice slightly.

Neve grinned. "Oh, I think we both know, don't we, Tobias?"

We did. I swallowed.

"You see, when you showed up at my house this evening, I made Ruby go and check out your car. I was worried you'd have a camera or a wire or something, but she found this instead. The clip full and everything."

I looked behind me. Lumen was staring at the gun, seemingly frozen in place.

"Lumen, come here," I muttered.

"Lumen, don't take a step forward!" Neve warned.

Lumen blinked, but didn't move.

Neve laughed. "You should have stayed in your house. None of this would have happened."

"You wanted to kill me," Lumen said suddenly. She

straightened her spine and clenched her fists. "I wasn't going down like that."

"It doesn't really matter now. I'm the one with the gun. What do you have?"

Nothing. Lumen had nothing to defend herself on the ice.

"I don't need a gun to finish this. Come out here and fight me, bitch."

I blinked in surprise. Did those words just come from the timid, anxiety ridden woman I knew? Just hours ago, she was afraid to leave her house, and now she just threatened a woman with a gun in her hand.

"You think I'm dumb?" Neve laughed, but stepped closer to the lake. "I'm over this. It's midnight, let's get this over with." She stepped right up to Lumen, her gun still posed.

"Neve, no!" I yelled and reached for the woman, but it was too late. She pulled the trigger, and Lumen screamed and flew back, hitting the ice with a loud thunk. The ice let out a loud splitting sound as it began to crack.

Neve jumped up and down excitedly. "Fucking finally." She spun around. "Let's go."

I was too stunned to do anything but stare at the scene. Neve stood triumphantly, having shot my girl... with a tranquilizer.

I tried to focus my attention on Neve. I couldn't let her see my concern for Lumen.

"Are you ready?" I asked. "It is pretty cold out here."

Her eyes lit up like I'd just proposed. "Really? I knew if she was dead and gone, you'd move on fast. Oh, Tobias, you were worth all of this." She took a step forward just as Lumen lifted her head up. I rushed forward, stopping Neve from coming further up the bank. I wrapped my arms around her tightly, holding her in place, all the while looking over her shoulder, watching Lumen slowly stand.

"I'm sorry it had to be this way. I wish Billy and Ruby hadn't gone out like they did, but it was probably for the best. Now we can say I killed her for self-defense, and they won't question anything."

"You're so smart," I told her.

Lumen took a step forward. I frowned. She was dragging her right side. She'd been shot in that shoulder. Thankfully, my gun had been loaded with a dose for small dogs. She would just be numb for a bit. I locked eyes with Lumen, nodding ever so slightly as she slowly made her way to us.

"Are you happy, Tobias?" Neve asked. I looked up, just as Lumen was reaching her good arm out. I let go of the psycho that brought us here and gently pushed her back. Neve's eyes grew large with confusion as Lumen snatched her by the hair and ripped her backward, sending her spiraling onto the ice.

Neve dropped the gun and I quickly picked it up. This wasn't my fight. Lumen had to end this.

Lumen dragged herself slowly to Neve, and then just as Neve was sitting up, she dropped down on her middle, pining her to the ice. With her good hand, she reached for Neve's head again, gripping her head tight, and then she shoved it down, smashing it against the hard ice.

Neve screamed and fought against Lumen, but half of Lumen was dead weight, and she couldn't get her off her as she kept lifting and smashing her head against the ice. It was like hitting cement. Soon, a splatter of blood formed under her head where it kept colliding.

Lumen stood and kicked her further out. I wasn't sure

why she did it, until I saw that it was where she'd landed when she was shot.

Where the ice was cracked.

Lumen looked back at me, and I slid the gun across the ice. She picked it up and aimed it at Neve. Neve stood, and then laughed.

"You don't have the balls."

Oh, I think she did.

Lumen pointed at Neve's feet and shot once, and then again, unloading the clip into the ice.

"Ha! You missed, you stupid—" Neve leaped up in glee and froze as the ice made another loud cracking sound. Lumen scurried back, and I hurried onto the ice, dragging her back as the ice split and Neve dropped through an instant later, her scream cut off instantly.

We fell back onto the snowy ground and watched the water splash and bubbles appear for a moment before slowly disappearing.

"You're freezing," I said after a long moment.

"Nu-numb," she said through the side of her mouth she could move. I lifted her in my arms.

"Let's get you inside and in a hot bath. The tranquilizer will wear off in a few hours."

We trudged back through the woods, leaving Neve trapped under the water. We climbed the stairs, stepping over Ruby's burned body, and went back into the house. On the way to the bathroom, we passed the kitchen where Billy lay, candy canes embedded in his eye sockets. I massaged her muscles under the hot water, and cleaned the stab wound in her back, and the bullet wound in her front.

"I can do some first aid. These aren't as bad as I'm sure they feel," I assured her as I sewed her up with my kit from my car. Once she was clean, I pulled her from the bath, dressed her, and put her on the couch. I watched over her, monitoring her carefully. Once I was sure she'd be okay, I went to clean up the mess, starting with Billy.

I stepped into the kitchen and went to the speaker, finally shutting off the Christmas music. Then, I went around the island to where he lay, cock out and eyes gouged inward.

I left his body mostly untouched, but got his phone. Using his finger to open it, I deleted all traces of the video Neve had over me. I went outside and did the same with Ruby's phone. And then lastly, I found the tracker in Ruby's phone for Neve's location. Her phone was in the lake with her. This was a small town, no one would find her for a long time, and once they did, they'd just burn her and not ask questions.

I returned to my girl just as the sun was rising on Christmas morning. I greeted her with a cup of hot cocoa. She sat up, groggy.

"What—Tobias? Oh my god." She looked around frantically and winced when she tried to get up. "They're all dead, aren't they?"

"They are. I told you, I'm not going to let anyone hurt you ever again. Merry Christmas, Lumen."

I stared at the beautiful woman I'd been inside of numerous times last night. My cock was stirring again, pleading for her to still want me now that the sun was up. She stared for a long moment before smiling and reaching for the cocoa.

"Merry Christmas, Tobias."

EPILOGUE - TOBIAS

"I lied. There's one more thing." I gripped the wheel of my truck and turned toward the hotel I'd booked a few nights before.

"More? I'm ready to go home," Lumen whined. After we had hot cocoa in the morning, we called the police to tell them our version of events. Three masked people invaded her home, and she'd fought them off all night. When I arrived to surprise her for Christmas, we called the cops, who insisted we go to the hospital while they did an investigation.

"I know. Me too. I want to get things cleaned up as soon as we can. Thankfully they ruled it all self-defense and are letting you go back to everything."

"I don't know if I want to go back to everything." Her voice grew soft as she stared out the window.

"What do you mean?" I asked, pulling into the hotel parking lot.

"Well, going back to what I was doing before feels... lonely. I was trapped in my own mind, afraid to leave the house. I don't want to go back to that."

I parked and reached for her hand. "That's not going to happen. In fact, if you don't want to, you don't ever have to stay there again. We can move you into my place and sell this one. Whatever you choose, you're not going to be alone."

Her bright brown eyes lit up. "Really?"

I laughed. "Of course. Now that I finally have you, I'm not letting you go. You were my Christmas wish, Lumen."

I knew it was cheesy, but I couldn't help it. I needed her to know just how much I needed her. I'd never been this obsessed with someone in my life. I couldn't imagine a life where she wasn't part of it.

"Now," I changed the subject, "for your Christmas wish."

I hopped out of the car and hurried to the other side, helping her out. I urged her to lean on me as we went straight to the elevator.

"I got here a few days before, to make sure everyone was settled in before the big night," I explained as we walked to my room.

"Everyone?" She looked up at me. I grinned.

"You'll see."

I scanned the key card, allowing us entrance, and slowly pushed the door open.

"Daddy's back!" I sang to the room as tiny, excited barks flooded the room. I opened the door fully just as three little puppies ran toward us, nipping and wagging at our feet.

"Tobias! What is this?"

"These are my latest rescues. I travel the country, helping areas that have large number of unhoused pets. I get them basic healthcare and help find them homes." I scooped up the three Dachshund puppies and cradled them in my arms. "They are from the same litter; I couldn't bear to separate them."

"How did you know I wanted a dog?" She reached her hand out, letting the puppies lick her. I grinned. If only she knew just how much I'd obsessed over her this year. I knew everything there was to know about Lumen Morgan.

"Last year, I saw you looking at the puppies at the mall. Puppies are forever, but so am I."

Lumen took her eyes off the dogs and looked at me with such awe, such admiration, such... love.

"What do you say? Want to take us home? At least for the holidays?" I asked, adding that last part out of sheer nervousness she'd say no. My stomach tightened, worried for a brief moment her answer wouldn't be what I wanted. And then, she grinned, straining on her tiptoes to kiss me.

"That's all I want... forever."

THE END

ONE LAST THING BEFORE YOU LEAVE THE THEATER

Thank you for reading All I Want for Christmas is Boo. If you enjoyed it, please consider leaving a rating or review. Reviews are extremely important to authors and helps us continue to create books. If you do leave reviews, tag me on insta! (If you liked it anyways, lol.)

ABOUT THE AUTHOR

After watching *Heathers* and listening to My Chemical Romance one too many times in her teens, Chicana author, Tylor Paige, was drawn to the darkness where the villains were still villains, but deserved love stories too.

Shifting her focus to Horror Romance, Tylor writes slashers so sexy you'll be begging your partner to buy a mask.

When she's not writing about women railing the villains, she enjoys watching horror films, sewing, comic books, and participating in her local community theatre. At the time of this update Tylor has now written and published fourteen full length novels and four novellas.

Oh, and feel free to call her Ty. She prefers it.

ALSO BY TYLOR PAIGE

Final Girl Series:

Slash or Pass

Slay Less

Knife Comment Share

Final Ghouls series:

Hips, Lips, Apocalypse

Final Girl Featurettes:

(100 page horror romance novellas!)

Like Father Like Slaughter

Thots and Prayers: A slash or Pass mini sequel

Life Begins at Possession

Little Deaths: a Vampire Mafia series

Seven Little Deaths

Lay Your Body Down

Bury Me in Blood

Little Taste of Death (FREE VALENTINES SHORT!)

Standalones:

Surrender to Forever- a Goblin King dark reimagining

FIND ME ALL OVER

Www.Tylorpaige.com
https://linktr.ee/Tylorpaige
Facebook.com/Tylorpaigeauthor
Instagram: @Tylorpaige
TikTok: @authortylorpaige
Join the Tylor Paige's Whorror Babies group on Facebook!
https://www.facebook.com/groups/ 376190999768893/?ref=share
Patreon:
patreon.com/Whorrorbaby

Printed in Great Britain
by Amazon